MW00910674

Our Moon Festival
by Yobe Qiu

Illustrated by
Christina Nel Lopez

© 2020 | Yobe Qiu
All rights reserved. No portion of this book may be reproduced,
stored in a retrieval system, or transmitted in any form or by any means- electronic,
mechanical, photocopy, recording, or other- without the prior permission of the
publisher, except for brief quotations in critical reviews or articles.
Published in New York, NY by By Yobe Qiu Publishing

www.ByYobeQiu.com

Illustrated by Christina Nel Lopez

Paperback ISBN: 978-1-957711-00-3
Hardcover ISBN: 978-1-7355835-9-4

This book belongs to:

_____

From:

_____

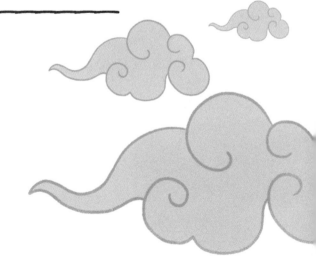

Zhong Qiu Jie

Chinese Mid-Autumn Festival

Today is the Mid-Autumn Festival! In Shanghai, we call it Zhong Qiu Jie. This year, my cousin Merry is visiting from Singapore.

Nai Nai is making mooncakes with lotus seeds, mung bean paste, and salted eggs. They smell delicious!

During the Mid-Autumn Festival, we give mooncakes as gifts to represent our best wishes for peace, health, and happiness.

My favorite part of the Mid-Autumn Festival is the delicious dinner! I love the extra-luck fish, soup dumplings, and roasted duck.

We read riddles from paper lanterns. Then Ye Ye tells the story of how Chang'e, the goddess of the moon, took the elixir of life and flew up to live on the moon!

t's time for mooncakes! Nai Nai brings out a plate fresh from the oven.

When Merry eats the durian mooncake, Ye Ye pinches his nose. We all laugh—not everyone likes the strong smell of durian!

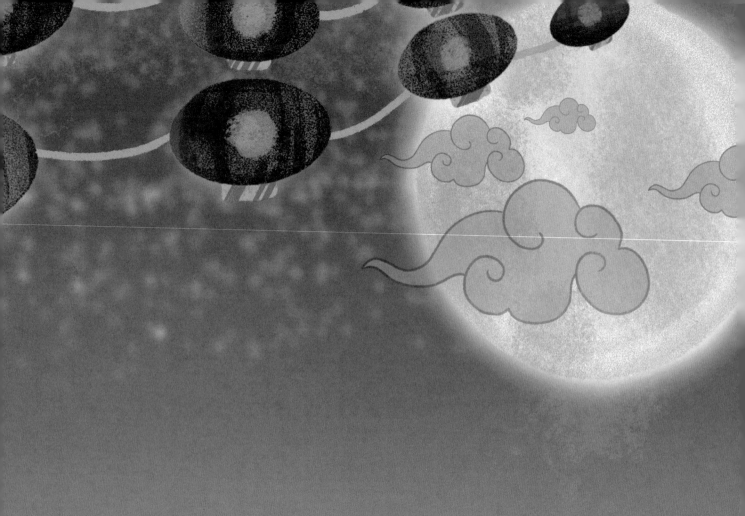

After dinner, Merry shows me the lanterns she brought from home. She says that many streets in Singapore are filled with glowing lanterns during the Mid-Autumn Festival.

We walk together with our lanterns to Yu Garden, which has been covered in bright lights that dance across the water.

Before we leave, I wave and say good night to the moon shining brilliantly above me. Sometimes I think I see Chang'e waving back at me.

Tết Trung Thu
Vietnamese Moon Festival

Today is Tết Trung Thu, one of my favorite holidays!
It is a time to celebrate the full moon, the harvest, and the opportunity to be together. This year I get to celebrate Tết Trung Thu with my family in Hanoi.

Uncle Keith is preparing the altar. He says we light incense to those who are no longer with us.

Grandma also puts mooncakes, flowers, and a glass of water on the altar. "Don't forget the spirit money, Mom," reminds Uncle Keith.

In the afternoon, Mom takes us to see a traditional water puppet show. Dad and I cannot understand the singers' words, but we are impressed by the puppeteers' skills.

We gasp when the fish jumps out of
the water and the baby phoenix
appears from the egg.

When the show ends, we walk around Hanoi Old Quarter. It is full of colorful lights, and everywhere we look there are children jumping rope and playing with lanterns.

We watch in amazement as the lion dancers and dragon parade come through the street.

At dinner, our whole family enjoys mooncakes and tea together. We open the window to admire the full moon.

Tsukimi

Japanese Moon Festival

Today is Tsukimi! It is a time for quiet reflection to celebrate the harvest moon. We are all looking forward to the special food that Grandpa made for tonight's solemn dinner.

Grandma puts the susuki plant in a vase by the door.
Dad says it will keep bad luck away!

Tonight, we will each share something we are thankful for.

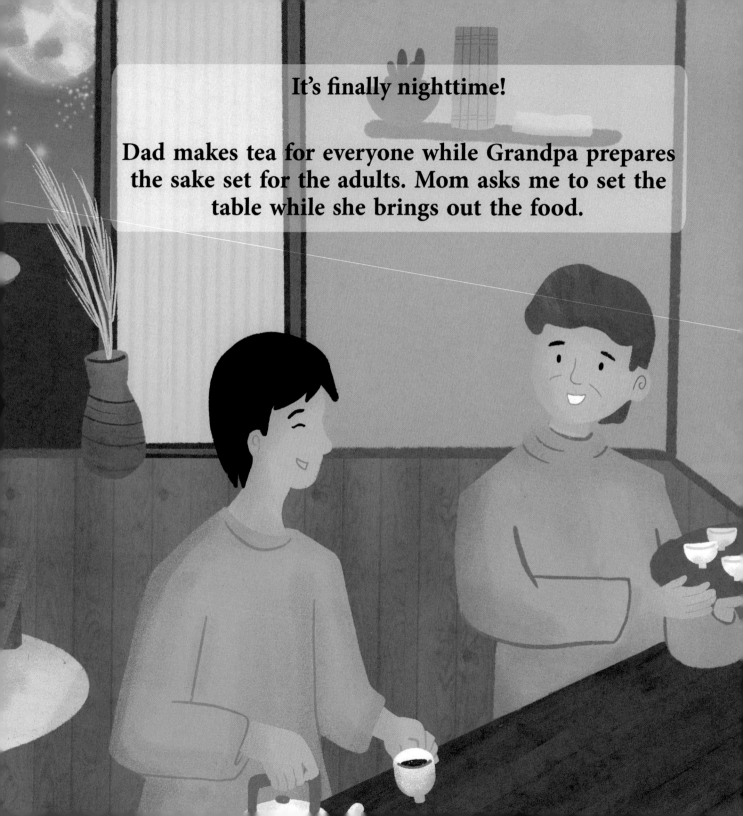

It's finally nighttime!

Dad makes tea for everyone while Grandpa prepares the sake set for the adults. Mom asks me to set the table while she brings out the food.

Everyone has a job on Tsukimi. We will eat outside in our backyard so we can appreciate the full moon.

Tonight, many families across Japan are enjoying dango and taro.

Tsukimi dango are my favorite—especially the chestnut ones! The round shape of the sweet, soft rice dumplings resembles the full moon.

On Tsukimi, our foods are offerings to the moon to bring about a good harvest for next year.

When we finish eating, I gaze at the moon to find the rabbit in the moon. Grandpa reads a haiku poem about the moon. Grandma reads one about peacefulness during Tsukimi.

We all admire the stillness of the
moon tonight.

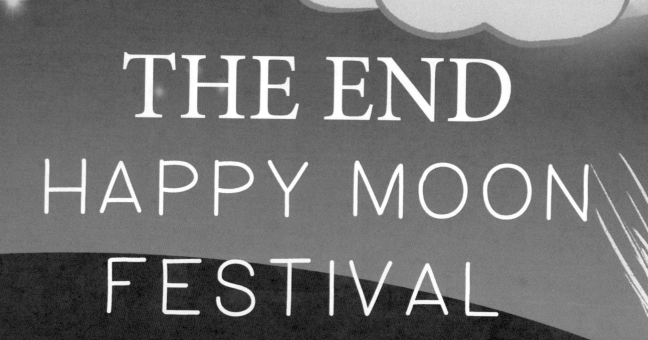

THE END

HAPPY MOON

FESTIVAL

About the Author

Yobe is a bestselling author, educator, entrepreneur and mom who lives in New Jersey.

For many years, Yobe focused on teaching children and families in her programs to embrace love, diversity and different cultures. She always dreamed of publishing children's books where her daughter will feel represented.

Yobe Qiu is the author of

Our Lunar New Year
Our Moon Festival
Our Double Fifth Celebration
The Asian Holidays Children's Activity Book
Asian Adventures A-Z

If you enjoyed this book, or any of Yobe Qiu's books, please leave a review. Your kindness and support are greatly appreciated!

Made in the USA
Las Vegas, NV
22 September 2023

77941036R00021